LAKELAND
FOLK TALES
FOR CHILDREN

LAKELAND
FOLK TALES
FOR CHILDREN

TAFFY THOMAS MBE

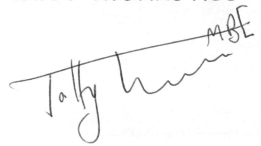

The
History
Press

First published 2016

The History Press
The Mill, Brimscombe Port
Stroud, Gloucestershire, GL5 2QG
www.thehistorypress.co.uk

British Library Cataloguing in Publication Data.
A catalogue record for this book is available from the British Library.

ISBN 978 0 7509 6611 5

Typesetting and origination by The History Press
Printed in Great Britain by TJ International Ltd, Padstow, Cornwall

For Ona and Uma,
my dear granddaughters
and for children everywhere.

A RIDDLE

To get into this book
solve this riddle:

My first is in king, but never in queen,
My second's in river and also in stream,
My third is in yes, but never in no,
My whole will open where you want to go.

Unlock the door and walk in.

CONTENTS

ABOUT THE AUTHOR

Taffy Thomas has been living in Grasmere for well over thirty years. He was the founder of legendary '70s folk theatre company Magic Lantern, who used shadow puppets and storytelling to illustrate folk tales. After surviving a major stroke in 1985 he used oral storytelling as speech therapy, which led him to find a new career working as a storyteller.

He set up the Storyteller's Garden and the Northern Centre for Storytelling at Church Stile in Grasmere, Cumbria.

He was asked to become patron of the Society for Storytelling and was awarded an MBE for Services to Storytelling and Charity in the Millennium honours list.

In January 2010 he was appointed the first UK Storyteller Laureate at The British Library.

He was awarded the Gold Badge, the highest honour of the English Folk Dance and Song Society, that same year.

At the 2013 British Awards for Storytelling Excellence Taffy received the award for outstanding male storyteller and also the award for outstanding storytelling performance for his piece 'Ancestral Voices'.

More recently he has become patron of Open Storytellers, a charity that works to enrich and empower the lives of people marginalised because of learning and communication difficulties, and also the patron of the East Anglian Storytelling Festival.

ABOUT THE ILLUSTRATOR

The illustrations have been drawn by young Cumbrian artist Steven Gregg. Steven was born and raised in the Lake District and currently lives in Windermere. He studied graphic design at Nottingham Trent University and is now working in freelance illustration.

When asked to work as illustrator for this book he commented, 'Cumbria is a county filled with magical places and eccentric people, all of which contribute to a wealth of imagery waiting to be tapped into for creativity, be it storytelling or illustration. Being born and raised here I am proud to be able to work with Taffy to help bring this collection of stories to life.'

FOREWORD

I have a rather unusual job. I make animated films.

I hope you've seen some of them: from very short ones like the *Amazing Adventures of Morph*, which may only last a minute, to middle-sized stories like *Shaun the Sheep* right up to full-length feature films like *Chicken Run* or *The Pirates*. Together with a whole studio full of people, we make beautiful puppets and sets, and we bring them to life through the magic of animation.

You may imagine it's a very complicated process and needs lots of talented people, each doing extraordinary things. But for all those people and all those skills, the single most important part of what we do – the very heart of it – is **STORYTELLING**. Without that we have nothing.

An animated film is just a story told in a particular way and watched on a screen. But in this book, you can go back to basics, to *pure storytelling*, with some beautiful illustrations of course. Because great storytelling is one of the simplest and most magical arts. You can read these stories to yourself, you can read them aloud to others, and you can remember them and tell them again in your own words. They're timeless, and yet they're perfectly modern; they can be told anywhere, and yet they belong to a special particular place – England's Lakeland.

So turn off those screens for a while – even if they are showing *Shaun the Sheep* – and listen, read and immerse yourself in Taffy's wonderful stories.

Peter Lord
2016

INTRODUCTION

'Lakeland can be appreciated by anyone who has an eye to perceive and a heart to enjoy.'

William Wordsworth

Even in the extreme flood conditions of winter 2015/16 , when the Lake District lost forty-eight bridges and a major road, and literally thousands of homes and buildings were flooded, many for the second or third time, the prime minister still described Lakeland as 'a jewel in the crown of English tourism'.

Approximately 16 million people visit the Lakeland counties of Cumbria every year. A third of these visitors are families. So what do they do when they arrive here from the cities? There are no theme parks and whilst there are some excellent visitor attractions, with mountains or fells to climb and scramble, and becks, tarns and lakes for swimming, sailing and canoeing, Lakeland is in fact its own natural theme park.

With its exposure to the North Atlantic, Lakeland can seldom promise fine or dry weather. Every year there is a handful of dry days with crystal-clear air and perfect light. It is this air and light that has attracted artists, authors and poets for more than 200 years, and it is some of the best works of these artists that continue to attract others to this day.

Local legends inspired the poet Wordsworth as did the landscape itself. The crystal-clear waters of the lakes and their mysterious islands inspired the author Arthur Ransome to write *Swallows and Amazons*. Author Beatrix

Potter, descendant of Lancashire cotton mill owners, left her home in London to settle in the Lake District and became a successful farmer. Inspired by the beauty and wildlife of Lakeland, she created a rabbit called Peter, a frog called Jeremy Fisher and various other enchanting characters. I'm sure families try and catch a glimpse of these creatures on their Lakeland holidays to this day.

Whilst this storyteller and author would not claim to have either the celebrity or literary prowess of Potter or Ransome, it is my hope that this collection of stories, gathered over forty years immersed in the beauty of Lakeland with farmers, shepherds and fishermen or just allowing my own imagination to run free, will find a place on the bookshelves of both visitors and those lucky enough to live here. These families may look for

Mr Coney on the riverbank, the dragon at Rydal Cave or even the swans on Grasmere's lake. On this treasure hunt you may also bump into a rabbit called Peter on a grassy bank or row next to swallows and amazons on a boat trip.

Because I am first and foremost a storyteller I speak directly to you, my readers, in the introductions to the tales that follow, and after each story title I name the place in which the story is set.

If you enjoy the stories please pass them on and share the love of this unique and beautiful part of England and its entrancing tales. Those who love this land will help to care for it.

Taffy Thomas
The Storyteller's House, 2016

ACKNOWLEDGEMENTS

For these stories to reach the printed page I am reliant on the help of a number of 'electro scribes' to whom I half tell and half dictate from the handwritten notes in my pile of exercise books. These helpers include my wife and muse Chrissy, my daughter Rosie, and Tony Farren. I hope this verbal communication between us allows my storyteller's voice to come through to you, my reader.

Many of these tales started their lives in the minds and mouths of Lakeland farmers, housewives and fishermen. In putting these together I have been a collector. Some of them, however, have been the construct of my own creative brain steeped in more than fifty years of the style and conceits of folk song and folk tale. It is the fact that my young readers are absorbing them and passing them on that makes them the next generation of folk tales from the storytellers of the future.

To everyone who gave me stories or ideas I am hugely grateful. As I grow older I am hopeful the stories will outlive me in the hands of you, my readers.

Nicola Guy and the team at The History Press have been, as ever, supportive. Children's author Helen Watts has been a writing mentor to me, as well as allowing me to use 'The Boy with the Harp', which was our collaboration, in this collection.

Steven Gregg returned to his native Lakeland after completing an art degree in the Midlands. Drawing on the culture and scenery he grew up with, he continues to produce illustrations of the highest quality that always delight and occasionally surprise me. Thanks Stevo.

In conclusion, none of my extensive storytelling performances, books or audio recordings would reach fruition without the selfless support of my wife, Chrissy.

The Dragon of Winter

SCAFELL PIKE

Despite the efforts of St George, every part of England boasts a dragon story or two. The tale that follows is one that I have brought home from my travels. It seems to live happily here, even changing to feature 'a host of golden daffodils', the Lakeland sign of spring.

It was the iron winter. The Dragon of Winter had curled itself around Scafell Pike, with its icy scales and tail sliding down into Lakeland and towards the Furness peninsula. The rivers Duddon and Greta were frozen solid; even part of the sea was frozen at Whitehaven and Maryport. Wastwater, the deepest lake in the country, was frozen so solid that the good people of Wasdale were able to safely skate on it from end to end. Ships couldn't sail into the port of Whitehaven with food from foreign parts. All the people who lived in West Cumbria fell on hard times.

They went to the pompous mayor and told him that he would have to do something about the situation. The mayor knew he would have to go and reason with the dragon and persuade him to fly elsewhere. He put on his climbing boots and warm clothes. Slipping and sliding he climbed up Scafell Pike, until he was staring into the icy blue eyes of the Dragon of Winter.

He told the dragon it was upsetting local folk as they were not getting enough food and they were freezing. Because of this the dragon would have to go elsewhere.

The dragon told the mayor he was reluctant to leave as he loved Cumbria and the Cumbrian folk, and especially his lofty perch.

Regretfully the mayor insisted that the dragon would have to leave. The dragon asked where he might go. The mayor suggested the dragon could fly to the frozen north and make a home with the polar bears and the Inuit.

A tear came to the dragon's icy blue eye. This was his place; he didn't want to go. The mayor, although pompous, was kindly, and realised a compromise was called for.

The mayor suggested the dragon could stay up on Scafell Pike for part of the year, the months that Cumbrians call winter. The time that the dragon spent in the frozen north would be the time that Cumbrians call summer. The time when the dragon was flying north would be called spring. The time that the dragon was flying back would be called autumn. That was agreed and the mayor returned down the mountain to the towns and villages, and told his people that the problem had been solved. They were delighted and told him he had done well, for they knew he had been very brave to climb the mountain and face the dragon. The following day the Dragon of Winter spread its white leathery wings, flew high into the sky and headed for the north. The day after that, the sun came out bright and strong. The fishermen could go out and fish from Whitehaven harbour and ships from afar could again bring food into the ports of west Cumbria.

All the people had smiles on their faces and all was well.

When autumn came it started to get cold again, and again the Dragon of Winter returned to its favourite place and curled itself around the peak of Scafell Pike. All the people were cold, but consoled themselves with the thought that the dragon would soon fly away. But when it came time for winter to end the dragon was still there. Again the people went to the mayor, and the mayor realised that the dragon had forgotten the agreement. Although the families enjoyed playing in the snow and wearing warm jumpers and hearing stories by the fireside, again many were freezing and starving. The fishermen and farmers were struggling to work and again food supplies were running short. Once again the dragon was to blame. He didn't seem to know when to leave the mountain for the frozen north.

A young lad in the crowd who always looked forward to the return of spring, when he could help his father with the lambs on their tiny hill farm, had a great idea. He knew all the signs of spring returning and knew that he could help the dragon to know when to go. He squeezed through the crowd until he reached the mayor. Boldly he shouted that he knew how to solve the problem. Everyone turned to look at him. The crowd doubted whether such a youngster could possibly succeed where the mayor had failed.

The mayor bent forward to listen to the boy's idea. To the astonishment of the crowd the mayor took the boy by the hand and together they headed towards the mountain and started the climb up to the dragon.

When they reached the top they were staring into the icy blue eyes of the great dragon. The mayor asked the dragon why he had not kept his promise to fly to the frozen north. The dragon replied that he was confused and did not know when to leave and needed help to know.

The mayor told the dragon that he had brought along this young farm lad who knew all the signs of spring, especially in the Lakeland valleys.

The boy bravely took a step towards the dragon, telling him that his favourite sign was when he saw fields and gardens filled with bright yellow flowers with trumpet heads called daffodils. From behind his back he held up a daffodil that he'd collected on the way up the mountain – a daffodil that had managed to push its way through the frozen soil looking for the sun. He told the dragon that once the flowers began to peep through then this was the time for the dragon to be gone and allow the fields to be full of the beautiful bright yellow flowers, for the vegetables to grow and new lambs to be born and skip through those fields. The dragon looked at the flower and, wanting to keep his agreement as he loved the time he spent here, thanked the boy for his help. He now understood. Promising to return, he spread his great scaly wings and flew north.

The unlikely pair made their way down the mountain to the cheers of the crowd below. They could now welcome spring at last.

Ever since that day, as spring is due to arrive, folk throughout the Lake District make sure that there are fields and gardens of bright yellow daffodils. A sign of the return of spring and the departure of the Dragon of Winter.

The Cat Fishers

GRASMERE

This delightful tale centres on the River Rothay, which runs through Grasmere village and close by the Storyteller's Garden. If you follow the riverside trail you will pass the barn where the cat fishers live.

If you look over the bridge into the River Rothay at Grasmere, you might spot brown trout or sea trout. If you walk along the riverbank, you may well come to an old barn. Now, that barn is the home of two pussycats. One of these cats is an old black cat, and he's a bit like me, because he's a storyteller. The other cat is a little white kitten – she's young and she's fast.

Every night, the old black cat and the little white kitten curl up in the hay in the barn, and the old black cat tells the little white kitten stories. Those stories are usually about how good the old black cat was when he was her age, because those are the kind of stories that parents and teachers tell.

The little white kitten got fed up with the old black cat boasting about how good he used to be. So one night, the kitten said, 'I don't want a story tonight. We'll go straight to sleep.'

The old black cat said that this was a pity, as tonight he was going to tell her how good he used to be at fishing. Then, in the morning, he was planning to take her down to the riverbank and teach her how to fish.

The kitten said he should skip the story but still give her the fishing lesson on the morrow.

The following morning, the two cats yawned, stretched and padded out of the barn and down to the riverbank.

The black cat demonstrated that, to tickle a trout, she should put her paw in the water with her claws out, and when the fish swam over her paw she should flick it out on to the bank.

He demonstrated this several times and then announced that she could fish in that spot. He, however, was going a bit farther downstream. He knew somewhere better to fish, but wasn't prepared to give away all his secrets at once.

Excited, the little white kitten approached the water's edge. She put her paw in the water with her claws out and, as soon as a fish swam over them, she triumphantly flicked it out on to the bank next to her. She was proud she had caught her first fish, because she was young and fast.

Downstream, the old black cat wasn't doing quite so well. He was older and slower. He put his paw in the water with his claws out, but when a fish swam over his paw he was too slow, and by the time he tried to flick it out on to the bank, the fish was away and safe under a stone. Although he fished the whole of the morning and the afternoon, he couldn't catch anything; he was just too slow.

As the sun started to dip behind the fell, he gave up and went back to see how the little white kitten had fared. Seeing him coming up the bank, the kitten stood proudly over her catch and arched her back in a threatening manner. This was her first fish and she was proud, and planned to savour it for supper.

She called to the old black cat, asking him how he had done. On hearing he had been unsuccessful, because he was too old and slow, the kitten started to laugh. The old cat pointed out that one day she too would grow old, and anyway his lack of success didn't matter because she had caught a fish and they could share it.

The kitten pointed out that it was her first fish and she had no plans to share it. So the old black cat reminded her that he had taught her how to catch it, and that every night he told her stories, so perhaps now *she* should share. The kitten again stated she had no plans to share.

And so the argument began. The two cats howled, yowled and hissed at each other. They made such a row that they awoke old Daddy Fox in his den on the fell-side, for the fox hunts at night and sleeps during the day. He came down the fell-side to investigate.

As soon as he spotted the fish by the kitten, he licked his chops, for Daddy Fox liked to eat fish, too. He complained that the cats had woken him up and asked what their problem was.

The old black cat explained that they were arguing about which cat should eat the fish for supper.

Daddy Fox offered to be the decider. First he asked who had caught the fish. The kitten proudly stated that *she* had caught it and so it was hers. The black cat said that *he* had been her teacher and so deserved his share.

Daddy Fox realised the situation was more complex than it had first seemed, but he had a cunning plan to resolve the dispute. He pointed out that they had quarrelled for so long, the moon was out in the sky. Now, we all know that cats sing to the moon. That is why Daddy Fox's idea was a singing competition: the two cats should sing to the moon, and whichever sang the best would be rewarded with the fish supper.

The old black cat boasted that this would be him, as he knew all the old arias and folksongs, and what the young kitten called music – rap and rock – was just a noise.

The two cats put their heads back, drew breath, and started to sing: '**MEEEEEOW, MEEEEEOW, MEEEEEEEEEEEEOW.**'

While they were concentrating on their musical skills, they failed to notice as Daddy Fox stuck out his paw, flicking the fish towards himself. He seized the fish and took it back to his den to feed his vixen and his cubs.

The two cats sang on for another half an hour: '**MEEEEEOW, MEEEEEOW, MEEEEEEEEEEEEOW.**'

When they stopped singing, they looked down but there was no sign of the fish … and no sign of the fox. All they could do was return to the barn and go to bed hungry.

That was one night when the old black cat didn't tell any stories at all.

The Farmer's Fun-Loving Daughter

TROUTBECK

The group of activities known as the 'Arts', which include storytelling and book reading, together with music, art, dance and drama, are an expression of joy and life. In most families, brothers and sisters can be quite competitive. There are lots of stories where the hero is a boy or man. I've found a story where the hero is a girl, although her two brothers are tidy and hardworking. So something for all of you in this joyful tale.

Somewhere in the heart of the countryside lived a farmer and his three children. He had two sons, who were intelligent, hard-working chaps. However, his daughter was a fun-loving partygoer. The farmer was in the autumn of his years – the time was approaching when he would die. He knew he had to make a will to say which of his three children would inherit the farm. He went into town and called on the family lawyer. He made a will stating that the day he was buried, each of his children were to be given £1; they would have to use this pound to fill every room in the farmhouse from the ceiling to the floor. But the farmhouse was enormous and had 161 rooms. This would be a test to see which of them should have the farm. He was safe in the knowledge that he had made his will, and a couple of weeks later took to his bed and died.

The day after his death, his three children took his coffin to the churchyard and buried him, full of tears. After the ceremony, as the family gathered in the farmhouse, the lawyer arrived to read them the will. All three were keen to know who would get the farm. The lawyer explained they were each to get £1: they had to buy something to fill all 161 rooms from the ceiling to the floor. Whoever could achieve this would inherit the farm.

The first of the intelligent, hard-working sons went out with his £1 and his horse and cart; he bought every second-hand feather mattress in the area. He returned to the farm and dragged the mattresses into the house. Taking his pocketknife, he slit the mattresses open and filled each of the 161 rooms from the ceiling to the floor with … feathers. The lawyer checked from room to room. It took so long to walk around 161 rooms that by the time he came to the last one, the feathers had settled and there was a gap between the top of the feathers and the ceiling. The lawyer told the lad he liked the idea but there was one room that wasn't quite filled, so he had failed in the task.

The second intelligent, hard-working son took a dustpan and brush and swept up all the feathers. He then went out with his £1, and returned with a cardboard box: it was a box of candles. He stood a candle in each of the 161 rooms and lit them. He had filled every room in the house with … light. The lawyer checked from room to room. It took so long to walk around 161 rooms that by the time he came to the last one, the candle had gone out and it was in darkness. The lawyer told the lad he liked the idea but there was one room that wasn't quite filled, so he had failed in the task.

That left the fun-loving party-going daughter. She went out with her £1 and returned with a small box containing a flute. She opened the door of every room in the house and sat cross-legged in the hall, playing a lively tune. All in the house started to smile and tap their feet; some even started to dance. She told the lawyer she had filled every room, not once, not twice, but three times. The lawyer was mystified and asked her to explain. She told him firstly she had filled every room in the house with music; secondly, everyone hearing it had started to smile, so she had filled every room with joy; and if you put music and joy together, she told him, you have *life* - so even at the time of her own father's death, she had filled every room in his house with life. The lawyer - and even the brothers - were so impressed by her wisdom and spirit, they agreed she should inherit the farm. Whether she gave up going to parties and became a hard-working farmer or whether she carried on partying, or whether she did a bit of both, you would have to ask her … for she is the farmer's fun-loving daughter.

Mr
Coney

AMBLESIDE, RIVER ROTHAY

Have you ever wondered why things are as they are? These days scientists answer a lot of these questions. In times past, storytellers explained a lot of things in 'pourquoi' or 'why' stories. There are others in this collection. The story that follows explains why rabbits have long ears and bobbly tails.

Many years ago before Noah was a sailor, in the Rothay Valley there was an animal called a coney. Now the coney was a little bit like a squirrel; he had tiny ears and a big long bushy tail.

One day Mr Coney was hopping along the bank of the River Rothay, which is the river that runs by the famous Bridge House in the middle of Ambleside. He had just reached the Stepping Stones when he spotted some small trout shining in the stream and wondered how he might catch one for his tea.

Who should come stomping down the river bank but old Daddy Fox.

'Ah! Mr Coney,' he said. 'I'll show you how to catch a fish!'

He waggled his bottom and flipped the tip of his red tail into the water. He sat patiently waiting for a bite. He was using his tail as a fishing line.

As soon as a fish nipped the end of his tail, he pulled it out gently, seized it in his mouth and strolled back up the fell-side to feed the fish to his vixen and cubs.

Mr Coney decided to try the same ploy. He waggled his bottom and flipped the tip of his white tail into the water. He was sat patiently waiting for a bite when who should come slithering upstream but Jack

Frost. The river turned to ice, trapping Mr Coney's tail.

He was stuck fast by the tail when who should come flying majestically over the ice but the heron, or as she is known in Lakeland, the jammy crane.

Being a friend of Mr Coney, the heron paused to help. She seized one of Mr Coney's little ears in her beak, flapped her wings and pulled, stretching the ear. Next she seized the other ear, flapped her wings and pulled so that Mr Coney's ears were so long they met over the top of his head. The heron then seized both ears in her beak, flapped her wings and gave an enormous tug. There was a snapping noise as Mr Coney's tail broke a few inches from his backside, leaving a bobbly tail like a lump of cotton wool.

Confused, Mr Coney shook his head, discovering he had long floppy ears.

He looked so different with his long floppy ears and his bobbly tail that all of the other animals stopped calling him Mr Coney and started calling him 'rabbit' or 'bunny'. When in time he fathered his own young, they too had long ears and bobbly tails so they were also called 'rabbits' or 'bunnies'.

So it was then and so it is now. However, if anyone ventures to a fur shop (hopefully they wouldn't in this day and age), and if they attempted to buy a coat made of the fur of this animal, the label on the coat would not say 'rabbit fur', it would say the word 'coney'. This reminds everyone of the story of how Mr Coney became 'rabbit' or 'bunny', a story that a man called Charles Darwin never heard.

The Rum
Butter Dish

PARTON

*A young girl lucky enough to have grandparents
who lived in Lakeland had very special holidays
visiting them. These visits would sometimes
uncover old stories that live here, giving her some
unusual things to eat or leading her to magic
places … even a smuggler's cave. This tale came
just from her helping to clean a strange old piece
of pottery.*

Grandma's cottage in the Lake District,
in the village of Parton, near Whitehaven,
was completely different from the flat
where the granddaughter lived in the city.
The city flat was quite sparsely decorated,
just the necessary furniture, a TV and
a few books. When the girl visited her
grandma her chores were always to help
dust, clean and polish the brass and china

ornaments that covered every shelf and filled every cupboard of the tiny cottage. Whilst doing that on one visit, the girl for the first time noticed a dish with writing on its side. The writing said:

Butter to show her the richness of life,
Sugar to show her the sweetness of life,
Nutmeg to show her the spice of life,
And rum to show her the spirit of life.

When the girl asked her grandma about the dish, she told her it was a Cumberland rum butter dish. When the girl asked about rum butter, her grandma told her she'd give her a bit to taste with her bedtime glass of milk. She went into the kitchen and came back with a glass of milk and a finger of Grasmere gingerbread covered with a brown sweet spread – rum butter.

The girl loved it, and asked why rum butter was special to this area and why her grandma had the dish. The old lady told the girl that if she put on her pyjamas she would answer all those questions with a bedtime story. Settling by the fire in her dressing gown, the girl listened as her grandma became a storyteller.

'In midwinter this coast can be bitter cold. In your great-great-grandfather's (my grandfather's) day, ordinary working people like him liked to warm themselves with a glass of rum on cold winter nights. The government in London, hearing of the Lakeland folk's love of rum, increased the tax on it, so folk up here couldn't afford it. They were so cold and miserable they started to smuggle it in from abroad.

'One night, a group of men including the vicar and your great-great-grandfather were waiting on the beach for a big three-masted sailing ship to moor in the bay. As soon as they spotted the ship through the dark and mist, they rowed out to meet it. A large sack of dark brown sugar was lowered down into the smugglers' tiny boat. This was quickly followed by a tiny package containing nutmegs, and a small wooden barrel of Jamaican rum. All this made the tiny boat wobble, so the smugglers rowed for the beach. As they unloaded the goods on to the beach they saw lantern lights heading along the shore towards them. It was the excise men, or customs officers. The smugglers knew they were in trouble. They rolled the barrel and lugged the sack up the beach into a cave. Shaking with fear, the men knew they had to hide in the cave until they saw the lantern lights going back along the shore towards the town.

'This was in the days before fridges were invented. The farmer's wife from the farm nearest the beach used that cave to keep her butter cool in the summer. She had a big slab of butter cooling on a flat rock in the cave. The smugglers were hungry. Luckily the vicar had brought a few biscuits with him. The men mixed together some of the butter with sugar, rum and nutmeg. It made the first ever rum butter. This was spread on the vicar's biscuits, which he shared with the other men. A couple of days later the smugglers were pleased to see the lantern lights heading away from the beach, north towards Whitehaven and Carlisle. The smugglers headed home with their swag, and of course a new recipe.

'Ever since that day, Cumbrians have made and loved rum butter, having special dishes made to give to children at their christenings. So that dish was my christening dish,' Grandma continued. 'After we'd eaten the rum butter, the dish was passed round for people to put money in for me. Wasn't I lucky?'

The girl thought she was lucky to hear the story, and took special care in cleaning the dish before going to bed, dreaming of smugglers, ships and Excise men with lanterns on the beach. The next day she would ask her grandmother to take her to the cave.

Farmer
Merryweather's Cow

SIZERGH

You probably know the old Russian story about the people of a community co-operating to pull up a giant turnip. In the tale that follows, here in Lakeland the villagers work together to save a trapped cow. The story ends with a homophone much loved by you and me.

Now I could tell you about the iron winter. In the iron winter the snow in the Lake District didn't melt until 1 July! When it did melt, the farmers had to borrow ladders to get their sheep down from the treetops.

But I won't. I'll tell you about the soggy spring, when frogs wore flippers, goats wore galoshes, water voles wore wetsuits and Farmer Merryweather's cow got stuck in the mud.

She was stuck in the mud from her bottom to her bonce.

Farmer Merryweather was worried. He took two hand-turns of her tail …

… and he tugged
and he twisted
and he pulled …

… but he could not pull that cow out of the mud.

Luckily Bessie Blood the Butcher was passing, and she came to help.

So Bessie Blood held on to Farmer Merryweather and Farmer Merryweather held on to the cow …

… and he tugged
and he twisted
and he pulled …

… but they could not pull that cow out of the mud.

Luckily Billy Bun the Baker was passing, and he came to help.

So Billy Bun the Baker held on to Bessie Blood, Bessie Blood held on to Farmer Merryweather and Farmer Merryweather held on to the cow …

… and he tugged
and he twisted
and he pulled …

… but they could not pull that cow out of the mud.

Luckily Patricia the Postie was passing, and she came to help.

So Patricia the Postie held on to Billy Bun, Billy Bun held on to Bessie Blood, Bessie Blood held on to Farmer Merryweather and Farmer Merryweather held on to the cow …

*… and he tugged
and he twisted
and he pulled …*

… but they could not pull that cow out of the mud.

Suddenly, there was a loud *snap*!

And they all fell on their bottoms in the mud!

All except for the cow who was still stuck.

Now if that tail had been a little bit stronger …

… this tale would have been a little bit longer.

The Magic Orchard

LYTH VALLEY

This fragment of a very old folk tale told to me at Brockhole National Park Visitor Centre, Windermere, is very relevant in a time when some people are having to use food banks to feed their families.

Fruit is good for you, and you probably enjoy eating plums. The Lyth Valley in the Lake District is famous for a slightly sour, tasty plum called a damson. Originally called Damascus plums, they were first brought back to this country in the twelfth century during the Crusades. Every January, Crook Morris Dancers and friends wassail the damson trees in the Lyth Valley. This year, 2016, I adapted the old wassail chant to one that they could use to wassail the damson trees.

Wassail the trees that they may bear
Many a damson bright and fair,

For the more or less fruit they may bring
As we do give them wassailing.

Wassailing invokes old magic. In the story that follows, it is the damson tree that is magic.

There was once a young girl who was very poor. Neither her father nor her mother had work, so some days that little girl and her parents didn't have a proper meal. Even though that girl was poor in this way, she was rich in another: she had good friends. She also had a precious thing, a yellow bag that was given to her by her favourite uncle. It didn't matter that this bag was usually empty. She lived next door to a greedy, selfish old witch, who had an identical yellow bag. This woman had cupboards so full of food that she couldn't have eaten it all if she lived to be 110. She was so selfish that some days she was tipping food into a rubbish bin while the hungry girl next door was looking over the hedge with her tongue hanging out.

One day the girl, clutching her yellow bag, was running down the road to the park to meet her friends. The selfish old witch, clutching her own yellow bag, was rushing down the road to the shop to buy even more food. With their heads down running, neither the girl nor the witch could see where they were going. At the crossroads they bumped into each other and ended up in a heap in the middle of the road. The old witch turned on the girl in a fierce threatening way, accusing her of knocking her over. Seeing the old woman's wild eyes and clenched fists, the girl grabbed a yellow bag and ran away. The old witch screamed after her.

In her confusion and fear, the girl had grabbed the wrong yellow bag. At the corner the girl realised the bag was jingling.

She was an honest girl from a good although poor home, and wanted to go back. However, when she looked behind her, the old witch was still screaming after her. No way could the girl go back; it wouldn't have been safe. She ran into an orchard. She ran up to an apple tree and said:

Apple tree, apple tree, hide me
So that the old woman can't find me,
For if she does she'll break my bones
And bury me under cold marble stones.

To the girl's amazement, the apple tree answered, 'No – try the pear tree!'
She ran up to the pear tree and said:

Pear tree, pear tree, hide me
So that the old woman can't find me,
For if she does she'll break my bones
And bury me under cold marble stones.

The pear tree said, 'No – try the damson tree!'

The girl ran up to the damson tree and said:

Damson tree, damson tree, hide me
So that the old woman can't find me,
For if she does she'll break my bones
And bury me under cold marble stones.

The damson tree said, 'Yes – wriggle down into my roots.' Clutching the yellow bag, the girl wriggled down into the roots of the damson tree.

She lay there shaking with fear, as the old witch huffed and puffed into the orchard. The old witch went up the apple tree and asked the question:

Apple tree, apple tree, have you seen
A little girl with a wig and a wag and
  a bright yellow bag,

Who stole all the money that ever
   I had?

The apple tree answered:

   I've not seen
   A little girl with a wig and a wag and
      a bright yellow bag,
   Who stole all the money that ever you
      had – try the pear tree.

So the old witch huffed and puffed over
to the pear tree, and asked the question:

   Pear tree, pear tree, have you seen
   A little girl with a wig and a wag and
      a bright yellow bag,
   Who stole all the money that ever I had?

The pear tree answered:

I've not seen
A little girl with a wig and a wag and
   a bright yellow bag,
Who stole all the money that ever you
   had – try the damson tree.

In the roots of the damson tree the young
girl shook in terror as the old witch drew
closer and asked the question:

Damson tree, damson tree, have you
   seen
A little girl with a wig and a wag and
   a bright yellow bag,
Who stole all the money that ever I had?

The damson tree answered:

Yes! I have seen
A little girl with a wig and a wag and
   a bright yellow bag,

Who stole all the money that ever you
   had –
And she went that way.

And the damson tree pointed a big
branch out of the orchard and over the
hill.

The old witch huffed and puffed out
of the orchard and over the hill in hot
pursuit.

After a few minutes the girl, still
shaking and clutching the yellow bag,
wriggled out of the roots of the damson
tree and ran home to her mother. She
gave her mother the yellow bag and told
her everything that had happened. Her
mother took some money from the bag,
went to the shop and bought some food.
So that was one day that poor family sat
down together for a proper meal.

As for the old witch, she didn't go hungry, for she had so much food in her cupboard that she couldn't have eaten it all if she lived to be 110. Mind you, she never got her bag back. I think that served her right for being so greedy. What do you think?

The Boy and
The Harp

GRASMERE

Most English churches today have floors made of stone or even marble. However, many years ago, as far back as the Middle Ages, the majority of them would have been far more basic, with simple, earth floors covered with rushes. So on festival and feast days, it became a tradition for the local people to bring fresh rushes to the church, which would be scattered all over the floor to sweeten the air and help keep the congregation warm and their feet dry. The practice was referred to as rushbearing and the children often played a very important role carrying the rushes in the procession.

In the 1800s, when stone floors became more commonplace in churches, the tradition of rushbearing all but died out. However, five churches – all in Cumbria, and St Oswald's of Grasmere among them – held on to the tradition, still maintaining it today by holding a procession followed by a special service in the church. In Grasmere, Rushbearing Day is the Saturday which falls the closest to St Oswald's Day which, in the year of the new Millennium – that is the year 2000 – happened to be the saint's day itself.

The following tale focuses on a young Grasmere lad who took part in the Rushbearing Procession in the years preceding the First World War.

This story comes from the picturesque Cumbrian village of Grasmere. It involves a boy, a harp, a special village festival and a war that was raging hundreds of miles away from the peace and tranquility of Lakeland. Appropriately, the story begins in a storyteller's garden: a garden belonging to me which happens to be across the road from a church, St Oswald's Church.

One hot August day in the year 2000, dressed in a buttercup-yellow waistcoat and a cream panama hat, I was leaning on the dry-stone wall of this garden, watching a procession passing by. The procession had woven its way around the narrow lanes of the village and was now passing my garden and heading for the church.

Anyone in Grasmere that day who was unfamiliar with the traditions of this Lakeland village might have wondered what on earth was going on, for the people, young and old, who marched in the procession were carrying strange-shaped sculptures crafted from reeds – or rushes – decorated with flowers. I had lived in Grasmere for many years, and knew that this was Rushbearing Day, a festival which had its roots hundreds of years ago, back in the Middle Ages, when local people walked together to their local church and scattered fresh rushes on the earthen floor, to purify the air and help keep out the cold.

As they passed by, the people in the procession laughed and waved to me, for me and my special storytelling garden were well known in the community. I waved back, admiring the rushes, most of which were fashioned into the shape of a cross or some other biblical symbol, such as a basket to represent the story of the baby Moses set adrift in his makeshift wicker bed on the River Nile.

However, one sculpture carried in the procession that day stood out from the others and caught my eye, for the reeds of this sculpture had been twisted into the shape of a harp.

By now, a small crowd had gathered on the narrow pavement on the other side of the garden wall to watch the procession, and if those people were wondering about the significance of this haunting, multi-stringed instrument in the rushbearing ceremony, I certainly wasn't. I knew the two people who were carrying it and I knew their story. Their names were Terry and Sarah O'Neill, and you might recognise their surname as being from Irish heritage. What's more, you might also know that the harp is Ireland's official symbol and has appeared on its coat of arms since medieval times.

But national pride was not the only reason why Terry and Sarah O'Neill were carrying a harp in the procession that summer's day, and as the procession made its way through the church gate, I began to tell the crowd of onlookers their tale.

'Over 100 years ago,' I began, 'there was born in this village a baby boy. His parents named him William – although everyone called him Billy – and they also gave him the rather grand middle name of Warwick. So his full name was William Warwick Peasecod.'

One of the little girls in the crowd sniggered. 'What a funny name! *Peasecod*!'

'Yes, I suppose it does sound peculiar, but that's only because 'peasecod' is a word that has gone out of use today. Once upon a time it was more commonly used to describe the pod of a pea plant.' I smiled and the little girl smiled back.

Then I carried on with my tale. 'So where were we? Yes! William, or Billy as he was known, was born here in Grasmere in 1898. He was a good son and, to his parents' delight, he was gifted with a charming singing voice. So when he was old enough, Billy joined the church choir. He could be found over there,' I said, pointing to St Oswald's over the road, 'every Sunday morning and sometimes on weekdays too, whenever there was a wedding.

'Billy was among those children who, when they were big enough and strong enough, were chosen to carry the rushes in the annual Rushbearing Procession. This caused Billy much excitement and was a matter of great pride to his parents. All they could talk about for days on end was what shape Billy's rushes should be and how they could make the sculpture.

'Then Billy's parents hit on an idea. As their family was of Irish descent, wouldn't it be grand if Billy's rushes were in the shape of a harp? Not only was this the symbol of the beloved land of their fathers, it was also a reference to the Harp of David from the Bible story in which David the shepherd boy – chosen by God to be the future King of Israel – is invited to play the harp for Saul, King of the Israelites. Like Billy, David was musically gifted, and his harp playing was so beautiful that it soothed the anxious king and gave him renewed strength for his forthcoming battle against the Philistines.

'So having settled on a design, Billy's father went to see the local carpenter and commissioned him to make his beloved son a wooden frame in the shape of a harp. When the frame was ready, Billy's mother went down to the shore of Grasmere to gather some rushes. Then she rowed out into the deep, dark waters of the lake to collect some fresh waterlilies.

'On the eve of Rushbearing Day, Billy's mother worked long into the night, threading the rushes in and out and all around the wooden frame, and weaving the lilies in amongst them. By morning, when Billy came down into the parlour to have his breakfast, the harp was ready.

'Billy's harp was the finest of all the rushes in the procession that day and his parents were filled with so much joy and pride as they watched their son carrying the harp into the church, that they promised to keep the same wooden frame and decorate it for Billy to carry in the Rushbearing Procession every year from that day forwards.

'And they did just that. Every Rushbearing Day, as Billy turned thirteen, fourteen, fifteen and then sixteen, he could be seen alongside his friends and companions in the procession through the village, holding his harp high up in the air and smiling broadly.

'But while the days in Grasmere remained peaceful and calm, life outside the little Lakeland village was far from either of those things, for the Great War had begun, and Lord Kitchener had put out his call for volunteers to fight the Allies' campaign on the Western Front.

'So not long after his seventeenth birthday, in 1915, Billy Peasecod exchanged his harp made of rushes for a standard-issue rifle and joined the Border Regiment as a signaller. After saying a tearful goodbye to his mother and father, Billy set off for France.

'It was the signaller's job to send signals and messages back from the fighting to the Company's headquarters, which meant that poor young Billy spent most of his days near the front line in the midst of all the action and, of course, the danger.

'Those long, terrible days in the trenches left Billy feeling a lifetime away from the green valleys and rugged mountains of Lakeland and from his solid, little, slate-grey home on the edge of the beautiful village, nestled between the River Rothay and the twinkling waters of Grasmere. But like King Saul, who found comfort in David's harp playing before fighting the Philistines, Billy took comfort in his memories of home, of singing alongside his friends in the choir, and of those special days when he would carry his harp in the parade.

'The war raged on. Two Rushbearing Days came and went and, watching the processions back in Grasmere village, Billy's parents dreamed of the day when their son would be back and carrying his harp once again. But sadly their wish would never be fulfilled, for on 5 November 1917, nineteen-year-old Billy was killed on the battlefields of France.

'Although they couldn't bear to part with the harp, Billy's mother and father could not face the thought of anyone carrying it in his place in the Rushbearing Procession – not in the year after he died nor in the summers that followed. So gradually the harp fell into disrepair.

'Eventually, Billy's parents grew old and, one after the other, were put to rest next to their beloved son in the graveyard at St Oswald's. But their story, and that of the harp, and of the young choirboy with the beautiful Irish voice who became a soldier, lived on, as one generation of Billy's family passed it down to the next.

'And now I have passed it on to you,' I said, lifting my panama hat and giving a little bow to my listeners.

A ripple of applause ran round the small crowd. Thanking me, the people began to disperse, some to follow the procession into the church, others to make their way off around the village to do a little sightseeing.

Only the little girl who had chuckled over Billy Peasecod's name hung back. Tugging on the corner of my waistcoat, she looked up into my whiskery face and asked, 'But what about those people? The lady and the man who were carrying the harp just now? Who are they?'

'Ah, that's a very good question,' I said, 'as the answer closes the circle in Billy's tale. They are members of the O'Neill family, Billy Peasecod's relatives. As I said in my story, no one felt that it was right to carry Billy's harp for a very long time after he died, but because it's the Millennium Rushbearing this year, which makes it a very special year, Terry and Sarah O'Neill thought it would be nice to remember Billy. So they had that harp specially made. It's an exact replica of the one Billy had.'

The little girl nodded. 'It's a good story,' she said. 'I liked it. And I think I would have liked Billy too, if I had met him. Is it okay if I tell his story to my friends?'

'Of course,' I said. 'I think Billy would like that very much indeed.'

The King of the Birds

HELM CRAG

Helm Crag towers high above the Lakeland Village of Grasmere. On the summit, a number of rocks have been naturally sculpted by time and nature into the shapes of a lion, a lamb, and an old lady playing an organ, when viewed from the right angles. These unique landmarks feature in the following tale, along with a golden eagle. The last remaining Lakeland golden eagle lives on a flat mountaintop ridge above Haweswater, known as High Street. From time to time, he can be seen soaring high above the Vale of Grasmere – just occasionally above the Lamb rock, or on top of the Lion rock at the summit of Helm Crag.

One day, the golden eagle was holding court, sitting in his favourite spot on top of the Lion's head up on Helm Crag.

'Me, I'm the biggest. I'm the best. I'm the King of the Birds. I'm definitely the best!' he cried.

He was a boaster and a poser. In fact, all the birds had grown fed up with him. He had got a bit too big for his beak! So they decided to bring him down a perch or two.

They went to ask the wisest of the birds, who of course is the wise old owl, known as a 'hullet' in Lakeland – as indeed it is in Shakespeare's plays. A baby one's called a 'yowlet'.

So they went to ask the hullet what to do, and the hullet said, 'Well, it's obvious. Tomorrow, all the birds of the air must gather on the top of Helm Crag and when I say, "On your marks. Get set. Go", you must all take off. Whichever bird can fly the highest is the King of the Birds.'

When the birds told the eagle about the challenge, the eagle said, 'Well, that's a waste of time. It'll be me. I'm the biggest and I'm the best.'

The birds looked at the hullet and said, 'You see, there's the problem.'

'Leave it to me,' the hullet replied.

So the following morning, all the birds of the air gathered on the top of Helm Crag. The hawk posse gathered on top of the Lion. There on the Lion's head was the golden eagle, and there was the kestrel, the sparrowhawk, the falcon and the osprey. And as soon as they gathered there, the eagle started boasting: 'What a waste of time! Me, I'm the biggest. I'm the best.'

Perched on the rock known as the Lamb, right next to the hawks, were the big black birds: the rook, the raven, the jackdaw and the crow. And just a little bit farther along the crag, on top of the rock called the Organ, were the small birds: the robins, the blue tits, the great tits, the finches and a long line of sparrows.

Then a cacophony announced the arrival of the chattering magpies. They found a rock to land on, and were still chattering as they landed:

One for sorrow,
Two for joy,
Three for a girl,
Four for a boy,
Five for silver,
Six for gold,
Seven for this story which has to be told.

Incidentally, some say that the last line of this rhyme should be 'seven for a secret', but you shouldn't tell secrets, whereas you *should* tell stories.

As soon as all the birds had gathered there on the crag, the eagle started again: 'What a waste of time! Me, I'm the biggest. I'm the best.'

And the hullet said, 'Just a minute.' He tiptoed along the line right to the end of the Organ, and there on the pipe of the Organ was the last to arrive, the smallest bird of all, the little jenny wren.

The hullet whispered something in the wren's ear.

The wren just nodded then she turned and hopped all the way along the Organ and the Old Lady, hopped through the legs of the big black birds, and all the way round to the hawk posse. Then she climbed on the back of the golden eagle. She was so tiny that the eagle didn't feel the tickling as she nuzzled down in his feathers.

The hullet went back three steps and said, 'On your marks. Get set. Go!'

They all took to the air until the sky above Grasmere was black with birds. Indeed, they cast a shadow over Ambleside which has remained to this day.

All the birds soared high in the air, but the big black birds shot up faster than the rest. They had found a thermal. It was early summer, and as the air hit the warm rocks of the fells, it heated up. And of course hot air rises, so that draught of hot air lifted the big black birds – the rook and the raven, the jackdaw and the crow, and the hawks – until they were sailing up high above Helm Crag and Calf Crag, sailing high above the fells. As long as they stayed in that draught of warm air, they were fine.

But the small birds – the robins, the blue tits, the great tits, the finches and the sparrows – they started to tire. They drifted out of the warm air and hit the cooler air, and as soon as they hit the cooler air they started to come down.

They started to fall.

They started to descend.

And they landed back on the top of the Lamb, on the top of Helm Crag, back where they had started.

The next to come down were the magpies, still chattering all the way down:

One for sorrow,
Two for joy,
Three for a girl,
Four for a boy,
Five for silver,
Six for gold,
Seven for this story which has to be told.

They landed back on their rock and they looked up to the sky. There they could see the big, black birds, the rook, the raven, the jackdaw and the crow, still riding the thermal, sailing gracefully above the mountains and above the fells.

Soon they too had started to tire. They drifted out of the warm air, hit the cooler air, and they started their descent. As they came down, they landed back on top of the Lamb, on the top of Helm Crag.

That just left the hawk posse high in the air, soaring up there as only hawks can.

But now it was the small hawks' turn to begin to tire – the falcon, the kestrel, the sparrowhawk, and even the osprey. They drifted sideways, and as soon as they hit the cooler air they dropped like stones. They came down and landed back on top of the Lion.

Together, all the birds looked up and could see just one speck remaining, high in the sky, and they knew that the speck was the golden eagle.

'Well, he might be a boaster and a poser, but he was right,' they agreed. 'He is the biggest. He is the best. He's still up there.'

At that moment, the golden eagle also started to tire. Certain that he had proved his point, he drifted sideways, hit some cooler air, and started to come down.

On his back, the little jenny wren felt the change in altitude and, as the eagle started to come down, she launched herself upwards. So for that one wonderful moment, the wren was going up while the eagle was coming down.

The eagle landed back on the Lion's head. He turned and called out to all of the birds, even those perched on the Old Lady Playing the Organ, 'You see! I'm the biggest. I'm the best. I'm the King of the Birds!'

And all the birds said, 'But there's still someone up there!'

The eagle looked up and, sure enough, there was a tiny, tiny speck, high in the sky – the speck that you know was little jenny wren. He let out a big gasp.

They all watched as the little jenny wren drifted very slowly down and landed on top of the Old Lady's head, behind the Organ, then they all called across to her, 'You see, jenny wren! You are the King of the Birds, because although you are the smallest in size, you are the biggest in wit.' The wren was so pleased she started to sing.

THE WREN SONG

The wren, the wren is King of the Birds.
St Stephen's Day she was stuck in the furze.
Although she was little, her wit it was great.
If you boast like an eagle, you might share
  his fate.

The Ghost of Grasmere Gables

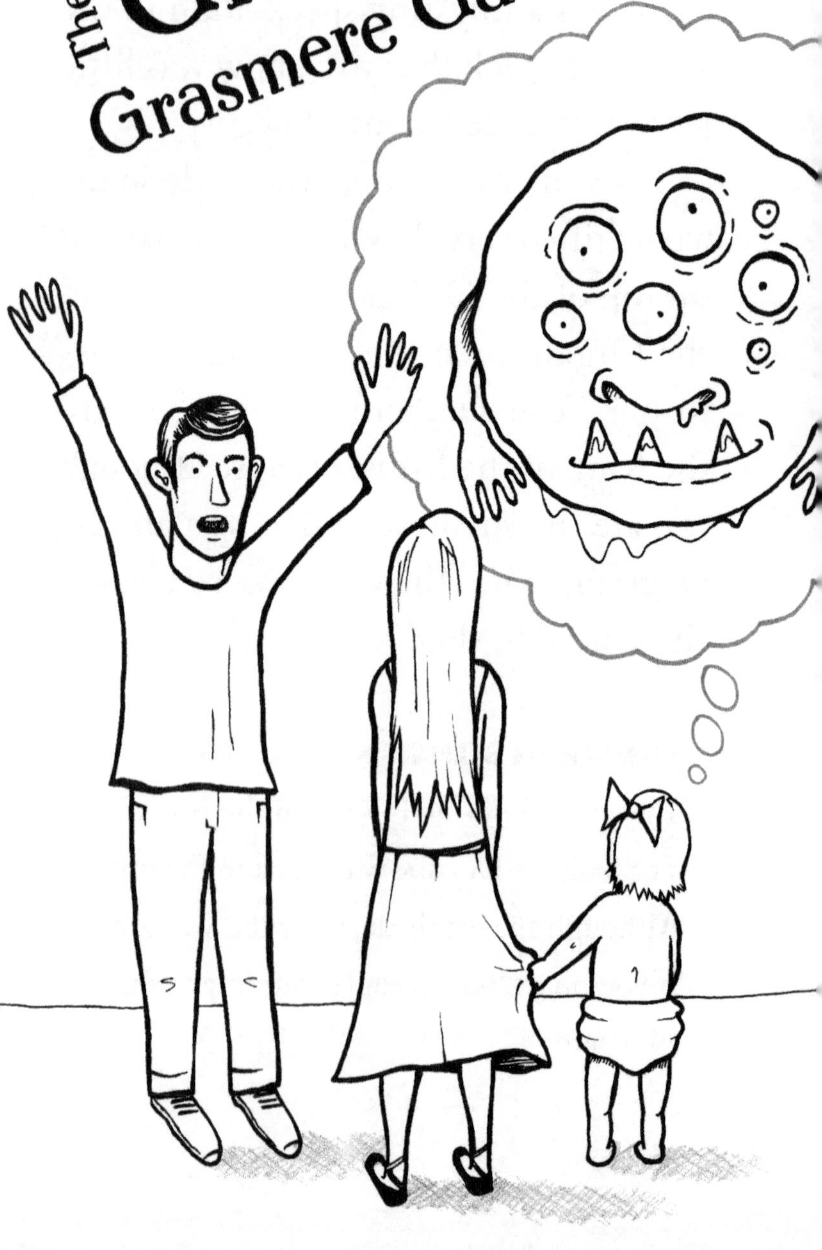

RED BANK, GRASMERE

Our popular Halloween event in Grasmere at the Storyteller's Garden would not be complete without the story that follows. You might like to make it part of your family Halloween.

Halfway up Red Bank, the steep hill between Grasmere and Langdale, stands a big old house called Dale End. The roof has pointed, sticking-up bits called gables, so people who live in the area know the house by the name of Grasmere Gables. These locals know two things about Grasmere Gables: first, it's haunted, and secondly, there's treasure there! This story is about three great heroes who went to get the treasure from Grasmere Gables.

Now, you need to know a bit about these three great heroes. The oldest one was a boy about sixteen years old. Like many teenage boys, he spent hours in front of the mirror doing his hair. The worst thing that could happen to him would be a Bad Hair Day. He was also desperate for money, to save up for a new skateboard. He had two sisters. The older sister was 14; she was always pinching make-up from her mother's make-up tray and needed money for the latest music or fashion item. These two teen-agers had a toddler sister; she was still wearing a nappy. This nappy was pointed, like a bumblebee's tail, and if you were lucky the pointed bit was empty. As yet not troubled by fashion or the need for money, the toddler went to the playgroup in Grasmere. This nursery was run by a wonderful, jolly woman called Mrs Happy. Now Mrs Happy taught the little ones that there was nothing to be frightened of in the dark, as there was nothing there in the dark that wasn't there in the light. For this reason alone, the toddlers of Grasmere knew no fear.

One misty evening, these three children set out to get the treasure from Grasmere Gables. The mist was hanging waist-deep as they walked up Red Bank. In the swirling mist the shape of the old house towered above them. They paused at the two stone gateposts that marked the end of the drive, to discuss who was going in first. Of course the 16-year-old brother said it had to be him. He felt he had to prove to his sisters that he was cool and hard. The girls were happy to hold hands and watch their big brother disappear towards the front door of the house. Although he told them he wasn't frightened, they could hear his knees knocking together like coconut shells.

Beyond their sight the big lad pushed open the heavy oak front door with the big iron knocker. A cobweb fell on to his head, spoiling his hairstyle. It was now a Bad Hair Day. Pulling the cobweb off, he squeezed through the door and then through the first door on the right, into the kitchen. There was a big wooden table, piled high with bags of treasure.

He was just about to help himself to the treasure when he shivered, and the hairs on the back of his neck stood on end, as he heard a weird, shaky voice: 'Oooooooohhhhhh – I am the Ghost of Grasmere Gables, and I say the treasure stays on the table.' This was followed by a terrifying scream.

The lad ran out of the kitchen, through the wooden door and down the drive. He had a problem, as he couldn't let his sisters know he was scared. They knew he was coming – they'd heard the scream. He ran up to them, quaking with fear but trying not to.

He just managed to blurt out, 'It was gruesome. It was a big purple bogey! It had teeth like daggers and eyes like fires. Blood dripped from its teeth and snot dripped from its nose. It was awesome!'

Never to be seen as less than her brother, the 14-year-old sister announced that she would go in and get the treasure. She left the toddler trying to calm down her big brother, and set off up the gravel path towards the big oak door with the heavy iron knocker. She pushed the door open, anda cobweb fell on to her face, sticking to the make-up she'd borrowed from her mother's make-up tray only that morning. She pulled the cobweb away from her eyes, and the mascara came off with it. Squeezing through the door, she turned right into the kitchen. There was the big wooden table piled high with the bags of treasure. Thinking she could buy make-up of her own, or even a new pair of trainers, she was just about to grab the treasure when she started shaking.

As her hair stood on end, she heard it: 'Oooooooohhhhhh – I am the Ghost of Grasmere Gables, and I say the treasure stays on the table.' This was followed by a blood-curdling scream.

Terrified, the girl shot out of the kitchen, through the big door and down the drive. She had to try not to let the toddler know she was frightened. Her brother and sister knew she was coming – they heard the scream. She ran up, shaking, and blurted out, 'It was gruesome. It was a big purple bogey! It had teeth like daggers and eyes like fires. Blood dripped from its teeth and snot dripped from its nose. It was awesome!'

The toddler told her sister that Mrs Happy had taught her at playgroup that there was nothing to be frightened of in the dark, and that she would go and get the treasure. She hitched up her pointed, bumblebee-shaped nappy and with her podgy legs toddled off up the drive towards the big wooden door with the iron knocker. She was tiny, and didn't quite have the strength to push the door open. She went back three steps and shoulder-barged the door, causing it to open a little. She realised that if she pressed in the pointed bit at the back of her nappy she could just about squeeze through the gap into the house. She pressed in the pointed nappy, but because she was a bit scared it was squidgy and not empty – poo! Holding her nose she turned right into the kitchen. There was the big wooden table piled high with the bags of treasure. By standing on tip-toes the toddler could just get her podgy fingers and saucer eyes up over the edge of the table to see the treasure.

She was about to reach for the treasure when the hairs on her neck stood up as she heard it: 'Oooooooohhhhhh – I am the Ghost of Grasmere Gables, and I say the treasure stays on the table.'

With confidence above her age, the toddler shouted back, 'I am a toddler from Mrs Happy, and I say the treasure goes in my nappy!' Grasping the treasure and stuffing it into her nappy, she toddled out of the kitchen, through the door and down the drive, to share it out with her big brother and big sister.

Imagine their joy as, holding the toddler's hands between them, the three great heroes skipped back down the hill towards the village.

The Hunchback & the Swan

GRASMERE LAKE

This magical story is perfect for sharing with family and friends on the shores of Grasmere lake. I have done so many times, and on more than one occasion have paused during the telling of the tale to notice two resident mute swans swimming towards me to listen. Now that's magic!

On the fell-side, near the lake in Grasmere, is a little thatched cottage. Many years ago in that cottage there lived a hunchback – an old man with a hump on his back; an old man so ugly that the people in the village would have nothing to do with him. Furthermore, the hunchback was completely mute.

But even though he didn't have any friends in the village, he did have some friends: his friends were the animals of the forest. So sometimes, when he went collecting sticks, the hunchback was followed by a line of animals – the weasel, the rabbit, the badger, the fox and, flying overhead, the robin and the wren.

The hunchback also had one very special friend, and that was a swan that lived down on the lake. He so loved the swan that, although he could not speak her name out loud, he called her his 'lady of the lake'. Sometimes the swan waddled after him and he'd half turn and stroke her beautiful curved neck.

Now one winter, the hunchback disappeared. Was he alive or was he dead? The people in the village didn't care, but the animals cared because they weren't getting their breadcrumbs and their saucers of milk. So the animals went to find out.

Off went the line of animals – the weasel, the rabbit, the badger, the fox and, flying overhead, the robin and the wren – off up the lane towards the hunchback's cottage. They made a circle around the cottage as the robin fluttered up to the window to peep in.

The hunchback was lying on the bed, completely still, and the robin whispered back to the other animals, 'I think he may be dead!'

Just then, the robin tapped his little yellow beak three times on the window and the flicker of a smile spread across the hunchback's face.

Excited, the robin reported back, 'No, he's still alive but he's desperately sick.'

The animals knew they needed help. They needed the help of the wisest of birds, the wise old owl, or to give it its Lakeland name, the hullet.

The robin flew off to the wood to where the hullet was perched on a branch.

Settling next to the owl, the robin reported the details of the hunchback's sickness.

The hullet advised the robin that if the hunchback got a visit from his special friend, his lady of the lake, it may cure him.

Thanking the hullet, the robin flew off to the lake where the swan was settled in her nest. Landing next to the swan, he told her of the hunchback's sickness, adding the owl's advice that a visit from her might be able to save the old man.

Immediately, the swan climbed from the nest and swam to the other bank. Then she started to waddle up the path towards the hunchback's cottage.

So there was the swan, followed by the line of animals – the weasel, the rabbit, the badger, the fox and, flying overhead, the robin and the wren. The animals formed a circle around the cottage – a magic circle.

As the swan waddled up to the back door and pushed it open with her yellow bill, the wren fluttered up to the window to peep in.

The hunchback was still lying on the bed. His face was as white as the sheet he was lying on and he was completely motionless.

The wren whispered to the others, 'It may be too late,' followed by, 'No, wait a minute. The lady of the lake is waddling over to the bed.'

The swan tapped her yellow bill three times on the hunchback's forehead and he started to smile.

Excited, the wren reported, 'We're in time! He's still alive!'

Just then, the swan tore some of the feathers from her left wing and jabbed them through the skin of the hunch-back's left arm where they remained.

Mystified, the wren reported this to the other animals.

Then, the swan tore some of the feathers from her right wing and jabbed them through the skin of the hunchback's right arm, where again they stayed. Again, the wren reported what he had seen.

On hearing this, the circle of animals became very agitated and asked, 'What's happening now?'

The wren reported that the hunchback had rolled over and the swan had torn some feathers from her back and jabbed them through the skin of the old man's back.

Inside the cottage, the swan then started to stroke the hunchback's hump with her yellow bill and, to the wren's amazement, the old man's back flattened out. Then, as the swan stroked the hunchback's neck with her bill, his neck became long and curved.

Everything had gone eerily quiet and the animals wondered what was happening. The wren informed them that they would just have to be patient and wait.

After some magical time, the back door of the cottage opened and, to the animals' amazement, out came not one but two swans. The swans waddled down to the lake, slid into the water and swam off side by side.

They say our friend the hunchback will be with his lady of the lake forever now, because swans, like most waterfowl, only mate once in their lifetime, and when they do they mate for life!

However, strangely, since that day, most of the swans in the Lake District are mute … just like the hunchback in our story.

The Star Apple

CARLISLE CASTLE

We all love riddles and try to solve them for fun. The princess in the tale that follows has to solve a riddle to escape from a dungeon. Perhaps you can visit the dungeon at Carlisle Castle.

Some people say stories are magic. If, like the princess in my tale, you cut an apple in half and find a star shape, it is magic! Try it yourself after you've enjoyed the story.

One fine day the princess was walking back across the field towards her castle, Carlisle Castle. As she got closer to the castle moat, the ground seemed to tremble and shake. The earth cracked open in front of her and out of the crack in the earth jumped a fearsome ogre.

'**AAAAAAARGH**!' The ogre seized the princess by the hair and dragged her away, across the field, up the hill into his gloomy old house and threw her into the dungeon. She lay on the cold stone floor of her cell, quaking with fear. The ogre stood over her menacingly. He snarled at her that he had some bad news ... and some worse news! The bad news was that she was his prisoner and the worse news was that if she couldn't solve his riddle, she'd be his prisoner for the rest of her days.

Once the princess had calmed down and collected herself, she wasn't quite so scared. After all, she was a smart lass, she enjoyed riddles, and was rather good at solving them. She was determined to outwit this ogre and get back safely to Carlisle Castle. Defiantly, she asked for the riddle.

The ogre told her that when he returned the following morning, she would have to give him: 'A golden box without a lid, and deep inside a star is hid.' Sitting on the cold stone floor, the princess looked around the cell in desperation; it was completely empty. Digging deep into her mind, she realised a box can be any shape or any weight as long as it contains objects. She thought of her round jewellery box and her Grandma's pill box. Time to explore.

The princess stood up and walked to the far end of her cell; there was a barred window. On the other side of the bars a tree was growing. It had but one branch; rocking gently on the branch of the tree was one green apple. The princess realised that the apple contained pips, so it was in fact a box of seeds, and didn't have a lid! But it had to be a golden box. She knew that there are many different varieties of apples. She had heard of Granny Smiths and Bramleys. Deep in her memory, she recalled one named … Golden Delicious!

The princess spoke to the tree: 'If you are a Golden Delicious tree, please bend down and help me.' Magically, the tree leaned forward, so she could reach through the bars and pick the apple. She realised that she was holding her golden box without a lid, for wasn't it a Golden Delicious box of pips?

Then she thought: *deep inside a star is hid.* What could that mean? She hoped the following day would take care of that and, exhausted, she curled up in the corner and drifted off to sleep, clutching the apple.

With the first light of morning, the ground started to tremble and shake.

The cell door was flung open and in leapt the fearsome ogre. '**AAAAAAARGH**!' Sensing triumph, the ogre asked the princess if she'd managed to solve the riddle. With quiet confidence, she handed him the apple, pointing out that it was a Golden Delicious, containing pips, and didn't have a lid.

Testily, the ogre said, 'But … *deep inside a star is hid*!' The princess fondly remembered times that she'd helped the cook make Cumbrian Rum Nicky (a kind of apple pie) by preparing the apples. With a mixture of memory and imagination, she pictured the centre of the apple. She asked the ogre to lend her his knife for a moment. Sensing defeat, the ogre handed her the knife. Carefully, the princess held the apple on its side on a stone, then she cut the apple in half across its widest point. Looking at the faces of the two halves, she noted delightedly that where the core had been cut in half and the seeds grew, they formed a star shape. She handed one of the halves to the ogre to show that she had solved his riddle.

After looking at it, the ogre ate the apple, for he knew apples are very good for you; after all, doesn't 'an apple a day keep the doctor away'?

The princess, with a smile on her face, ate the other half, for she didn't like to waste good food. Apart from that, she was quite hungry after her ordeal in the dungeon. The ogre told the princess that as she had been so clever in solving the riddle she could go free and return to Carlisle Castle, where – as we all know – the princess lived happily ever after.

LANGDALE VALLEY

This is a tale where the hero learns an important lesson. It is certainly a typical English folk tale that is 'at home' in Lakeland with its mountains, trees, steep paths and frozen puddles.

I have discovered that everyone loves this tale. Why wouldn't they when the protagonist falls on his bottom? That's funny – or so it would seem – especially if the person concerned has become 'too big for his boots'.

It was the iron winter. Jack Turnip sat in the grandfather chair in his tiny cottage and shivered. The hearth was lifeless and the log basket empty. His heavy axe stood patiently in the corner of the room. Jack knew what he had to do. He needed logs for the fire. He also knew that logs warm you three times: firstly they warm you when you wield the axe; then they further warm you when you lug them home; only then do they truly warm you as you sit by the fire.

Donning his hat and scarf, and with his axe over his shoulder, Jack set off confidently up the lane. Feeling strong and thinking of how much work he might do in a day, Jack didn't notice the frozen puddle on the path. He slipped over on the ice, landing flat on his backside! Collecting his scrambled senses he cursed the ice, regretting that it must be stronger than him – *or so it would seem*.

Then he pondered that although it was midwinter the sun would soon rise in the sky and gain the strength to melt the ice. Therefore the sun must be the strongest – *or so it would seem*.

Jack continued his train of thought. He pondered that even in spring, clouds could block out the sun, so the clouds must be the strongest – *or so it would seem*.

Then he reasoned that the March winds were so strong they could chase the clouds away. So the winds must be the strongest – *or so it would seem*.

Ahead of him Jack could see the mountain that overshadowed his tiny cottage. He pondered a little more that the wind couldn't blow away the mountain, so the mountain must be the strongest – *or so it would seem*.

On top of the peak silhouetted against the skyline was a hardy tree. Then Jack thought that a tree could grow on a mountain, but a mountain couldn't grow on a tree! Therefore the tree must be the strongest – *or so it would seem*.

Feeling the weight of the axe on his shoulder, Jack walked towards the tree and swung the axe, felling the fir giant in three mighty blows.

Jack stood triumphant with the axe above his head bragging to the heavens that he must be the strongest – *or so it would seem*.

Full of himself and more than a little hungry and thirsty, Jack headed full tilt down the path that led towards home. He was so much of a boaster and poser that he didn't remember the frozen puddle on the path. His feet went from under him and he fell flat on his bottom.

All he could do was grab a couple of sticks, crawl home and sit by his meagre fire pondering his mishap and vowing never to be boastful again.

The Valley
of Two Rivers

CARTMEL

Long ago a group of French monks had a puzzle to solve to find a place to build a beautiful church. Hundreds of years later, two visiting children each had to eat a lollipop to get two sticks to prove the story true.

Perhaps you could do the same, and follow in their footsteps if you are near the village of Cartmel.

One lovely Lakeland day, twins – a boy and a girl – were taken to Cartmel for the day to hear the man dressed in yellow with the straw hat – the storyteller – tell a story in the square. The children were excited, for apart from the joy of a new story, this outing would involve nice things to eat. They knew the sticky toffee pudding shop stands in the square along with a number of places where ice cream could be bought; and it was a hot summer's day.

Parking their car next to the great church that is Cartmel Priory, the family wandered into the square and joined the crowd gathered around the man in yellow. Raising his straw hat in welcome, the white-bearded storyteller leaned on his walking stick with the 'badger head' handle and began his tale.

Six hundred years ago an abbot called Bernard brought a group of monks with him from France to Lakeland to build a great church. Camping on the top of a hill, they started to dig the foundations for a large stone building. Every evening after their work they prayed together.

One night, praying for help with their mission, they were amazed to hear a voice from the heavens. The voice told them that they were building in the wrong place. Continuing, the voice told them they needed to find a piece of land between two rivers that flowed in opposite directions. The monks realised this would be impossible as all rivers flow to the sea. Bernard told his men they had to prove themselves worthy of this seemingly impossible task, as the voice they had heard was the voice of God.

They set out and searched the whole of Westmorland, the whole of Cumberland and the whole of Lancashire North of the Sands. Each day proved more impossible than the previous one. Pushed on by Abbot Bernard, the monks didn't give up, even when they found themselves back on the hill where their journey had started.

Thinking of giving up and returning to France, they again kneeled together in prayer. To their astonishment, they heard the sound of rushing water from the valley beneath them. Recognising this as a sign, they rushed down the hill to the village square, each grabbing a stick and tossing it into the river, expecting to see the sticks flow south towards the bay. To their amazement the sticks floated north, towards the mountains. Looking upwards the monks saw a great star, the North Star. This proved what they had seen. Rushing across the village to the site of what we now know as Pepper Bridge, the monks once again threw sticks into the river. This time they did flow south towards the sea.

Bernard and the monks cheered excitedly; their prayers had been answered. They set to work immediately to build the beautiful Cartmel Priory in that valley where they believed two rivers flowed in opposite directions. And there it stands to this day.

The storyteller raised his straw hat towards the Priory as the audience clapped. He told the listeners they could take little sticks to the bridges and see if the story could be true. The twins said that they would really like to try this, suggesting the best way might be to use lollipop sticks! Smiling, the grown-ups agreed. Before long, with lollipops eaten, one stick was dropped at the bridge in the square and the other on the far side of the Priory at Pepper Bridge. And, guess what? They both floated in opposite directions – as you will discover if you visit.

If you like this magical story, you might like to find out more about oxbow lakes with the help of your parents, carers or teachers, especially if they like geography.

The Silly
Sausage

GILCRUX

When you visit the Lake District you'll find it is not without reason that some people call it the 'Taste District'. A number of local dishes and ingredients have their own stories, literally 'stories good enough to eat!'

The tale that follows is about our much-loved Cumberland sausage. This is a dish and a story that delighted a group of young people in the Western Lakes, especially when I used my imagination to include a strange local competition, 'Gurning' or funny face-pulling, in the story.

I expect, after you've enjoyed the story, you could have a sausage for tea and try pulling a funny face. Give it a go.

Jack and Mary lived in a tiny cottage near Gilcrux in north-west Cumbria, just south of the Solway. Jack was a woodcutter and lived happily with his wife Mary. That part of the county is quite remote and you can but imagine the excitement that builds in the community as one of their annual celebrations, Egremont Crab Fair, the Biggest Liar in the World Competition or – more recently – Solfest, approaches.

Jack and Mary were excitedly waiting to visit Egremont for the Crab Fair, where of course the highlight is the 'Gurning' competition, in which brave locals put their head through a horse collar and distort their face in the most extreme fashion possible – yes, an ugly face-pulling competition!

Jack had always fancied bringing home the trophy to his wife, but he was far too handsome. No amount of stretching, straining – even removing false teeth – would distort his features sufficiently to win.

The day before the fair, Jack went about his business. He went off into the forest to collect wood, leaving Mary to prepare a nice Tatie Pot for his return. Just 100 yards into the wood, Jack heard a desperate wailing coming from a bush. Being a kind man, Jack parted the branches of the bush to discover the nature of the problem: deep in the foliage, Jack spotted a fairy in a bright green suit with a pointy hat and silver wings, with her ankle firmly trapped in a cleft of a twig.

Carefully Jack lifted the fairy out of the bush and stood her on a nearby tree stump. The fairy thanked Jack for saving her and told him that as a reward, he and his wife could have three wishes. At this news Jack leapt in the air with joy and decided he must race straight home to tell Mary about their luck.

On the walk home, Jack started to feel pangs of hunger. Now, that part of Cumbria is famous for its spicy pork sausage: Cumberland sausage. It was Jack's favourite meal.

As he walked up the path towards his front door, Jack wished for Cumberland sausage… in the kitchen Mary was just bending to put the Tatie Pot in the oven when to her amazement, there was a flash of lightning and a Cumberland sausage appeared and started sizzling in the frying pan on top of the cooker.

Jack excitedly walked through the door, shouting to Mary that he had some wonderful news to tell her of their new-found luck.

Mary pointed to the sausage, telling him that something strange was afoot. Jack told Mary of how he had rescued the fairy and been given three wishes. They could wish for anything they wanted.

Immediately Mary realised what had happened and asked Jack if he had wished for a sausage.

Jack had to admit his foolishness, at which point Mary pointed out that there was a perfectly good Tatie Pot in the oven and that he'd wasted a wish. In fact, she pointed out he had been so stupid that she wished the sausage was stuck to the end of his nose.

Well, just imagine: there was another flash of lightning and the sausage flew around the room before coming to rest and sticking firmly on the end of Jack's nose.

Jack squealed because the sausage was quite hot. He tried to pull the sausage away but it was stuck firm. He begged Mary to help him and … they pulled and they tugged without any luck for the sausage was stuck!

Mary offered to cut the sausage off with a large pair of scissors, but Jack feared this would mean she would cut off part of his nose, and refused the offer.

Jack pointed out that he looked more like an elephant than a woodcutter.

As if things weren't bad enough, the time had come for them to depart for Egremont, for the Crab Fair.

Well, it is said that behind every dark cloud is a silver lining, and Jack and Mary arrived at the fair just in time for the famous Gurning competition.

Mary entered Jack and – you've guessed it – with a Cumberland sausage stuck to the end of his nose, the face he pulled was so awesome that he easily won.

And so it was that Jack and Mary proudly took the trophy home to Gilcrux, with Jack vowing to head to Wasdale the following autumn to try and win the Biggest Liar in the World competition!

Although the sausage had been useful, in the comfort of their cottage Jack knew he could not live with it stuck to the end of his nose.

Mary reminded him they still had one wish left.

Together they held hands and wished that the sausage would come unstuck. There was a flash of lightning and the sausage flew around the room and landed back in the frying pan. Mary set to and made them both a sausage and egg pie, Jack's favourite. As for the Tatie Pot, like all good hotpots, that tasted even better the following day.

The Fairy Boots

THE STORYTELLER'S GARDEN, GRASMERE

The following tale begins in the Storyteller's Garden in Grasmere, where many people say that magical things can happen. After visiting the garden, you can take the path through the churchyard opposite to the bridge over the River Rothay. As you look downstream, it is easy to picture where the fly-fisherman might have stood, and where the tramp could have sat down to remove his boots.

Long before the Storyteller's Garden was created, the patch of land at Church Stile in Grasmere was a jungle where the grass grew long and plants grew wild.

One day, a tramp man, a gentleman of the road who had walked for many days without stopping for a meal, a sleep or even a wash, was walking out of

Grasmere and was passing by this patch of unkempt land. His feet were killing him, so when he spotted a particularly large tuft of grass his first thought was that it would be a nice place to take the weight off his feet, and maybe even to have forty winks.

He sat down and, because he hadn't stopped walking for many hours, he kicked off his boots and was soon fast asleep.

The tramp had been so eager to sit down that he hadn't noticed he was in the middle of a circle of toadstools: a fairy ring. And because he hadn't stopped for a wash he hadn't shaved either, so he had a stubbly chin.

After a few moments he was awakened by somebody pulling on one of his whiskers as though it were a tug-of-war rope.

'**OUCH**!' he cried, and he opened his eyes to discover that it was a tiny man in a yellow and green suit. 'Get out,' yelped the tramp.

'Get out yourself!' replied the fairy. 'You're in my place.'

'What do you mean, I'm in your place?' asked the tramp.

'This is the fairy ring and my king, the King of the Fairies, it's his birthday today. We're going to have a party right here. You're sitting where the band is going, and where your old boots are, that's where the food and drink are going. In short, you're in the way. Clear off!'

The tramp looked down at his worn old boots and saw that the tops had come away from the bottoms. A thought popped into his head and he said, 'If you would only give me some new boots, then I'll clear off.'

In a twink, the little man was gone.

After what may have been a second, or may have been a minute, the fairy returned, clutching a pair of bright yellow boots in his fingers. He popped them down by the tramp and said, 'There are your new boots. Now clear off.'

The tramp picked the boots up and examined them. He saw that they were buttercup yellow and every stitch was perfect, but they were only half the size of one of the tramp's thumbs.

Angrily, the tramp complained. 'Those boots are so small, they wouldn't even fit on my big toe.'

To which the little man replied, 'Try them. Those boots are fairy boots. They're bigger on the inside than they are on the outside. Try them.'

The tramp slipped one of the boots over his right big toe and the other over his left and, sure enough, his feet slipped right inside. The boots were a perfect fit.

Excited, he turned to the fairy. 'These boots are fantastic!' he cried. 'Where can I buy boots like these?'

The little man replied, 'Money wouldn't buy you boots like that. However, my king, the King of the Fairies, tells me you can have those boots if you make me a promise.'

The tramp nodded eagerly, so the fairy continued. 'You must promise me that you will never ever tell a soul where they came from. And if you do, the boots will disappear back to where they came from at the speed of light.'

The tramp promised, and, doing up the laces, set off towards the road.

'Oy!' The little man called him back. 'You've forgotten something. You've for-gotten your old boots.'

'But I don't need them anymore,' said the tramp man.

'Never mind that,' said the fairy. 'If you're in beautiful Lakeland, you can't leave rubbish lying around. Put the old boots in a bin or take them home with you.'

The tramp picked up the old boots and put one in each of his jacket pockets, and it was a good job that he did.

He set off down the road, walking faster and farther than he had ever done before. He didn't stop to eat, he didn't stop to drink, and he didn't stop to rest, even though it was hot midsummer. Nor did he stop to wash his feet and change his socks, so before long his feet started to smell. In fact, his feet ponged so badly that all of the cows looking over the hedge said 'poo' instead of 'moo'.

Now that tramp was more than 2 metres tall, so you can imagine how far his nose was away from his socks. But soon, even *he* couldn't stand the stench any longer. He was going to *have* to wash his feet.

The tramp looked into the next field and saw a fisherman standing waist-deep in a river, fly-fishing. The tramp thought that the fisherman would not be pleased if he muddied the stream, but too bad. He couldn't stand the smell any longer.

He walked over to the river, sat down on the bank and removed his buttercup-yellow boots, putting them on a stone. His socks were so rotten that they simply fell off.

The tramp dipped his toes in the water. It felt so good that he couldn't resist standing up and swishing his feet around. But this made the stream muddy.

The fisherman turned to tell the tramp to push off, but then he spotted the bright yellow boots sitting on the stone.

'Those boots are fantastic!' he said. 'Where can I get boots like that?'

The tramp replied, as the fairy had, that money could not buy boots like that.

'Well, whose are they?' asked the fisherman.

'They're mine,' said the tramp.

'But they're too small,' said the fisherman. 'They can't be yours.'

'Ah,' said the tramp. 'Those boots are bigger on the inside than they are on the outside.'

'Where did you get them?' the fisherman enquired.

'I'm not saying,' said the tramp.

The fisherman told the tramp that if he couldn't reveal the origin of the boots, then he had to assume that he had stolen them.

The tramp told the fisherman that he could assume whatever he liked, but he had certainly not stolen anything.

Then the fisherman announced that if the tramp would say where he had got the boots, he would leave him in peace. So, just to get the fisherman out of his hair, the tramp man told him the story of how he had come by the boots.

When he had finished his tale, the tramp looked up at the sky and realised that there was just enough daylight for him to walk another five miles. So he paddled back to the bank and bent down to put on his boots. But although he searched under the stones and in the grass, he couldn't find them anywhere. The boots had gone back to where they had come from.

All the tramp could do was to take his old boots out of his jacket pocket and wrap a piece of orange baler twine around them. Then he walked off down the road.

So, if you're in the Lake District and you spot a gentleman of the road wearing old boots with orange twine wrapped around them, then you know, as I know, that he once had a pair of buttercup-yellow boots but he lost them because he didn't know how to keep a promise to the fairies.

The Cobblestone
Maker

HONISTER CRAG

As a boy I was lucky to spend a lot of time with my grandfather who told me I was as good and important as anyone else in this world ... but no more so. This has been useful to me in my lifetime as a storyteller when I have spent much of my time with common folk, but also twice met the queen. The story that follows reminds me of my grandfather's wise words.

It is also the story I most use to teach new storytellers, as the pictures the words make are very clear and vivid, and the shape of the story is strong. I hope when you've read it once or twice you'll know it well enough to tell it.

There was a little cobblestone maker, who was the finest cobblestone maker in the world. However, he was unhappy. Whenever he did his very best work, all people did was walk on it. He wished that he could be more important, more powerful, and stronger.

So one day, he was chipping at a cobblestone, wishing he was more important, when to his amazement he discovered that he was wearing a crown and a red cloak with white fur around the bottom. All the folk in the street bowed and knelt down, believing that he had become a king.

The cobblestone maker thought *Great. Now I'm important. Now I'm powerful. Now I'm strong. My wish has been granted. My ambition has been fulfilled.*

Just then, the sun came out and all the people turned their heads to enjoy it. The cobblestone maker cursed. Obviously, he thought, the sun is more important than a king. So, if I want to be more important than the sun, I must wish to be a cloud.

So he wished to be a thundercloud, the strongest cloud of all.

There was a flash of blue light and the cobblestone maker discovered that he had become a slate-grey cloud, floating across the sky. All the people looked up. Seeing this dark cloud they ran for their umbrellas and raincoats. Just to make sure that no one had missed him, the cobblestone maker sent down a flash of lightning … followed by a crash of thunder … followed by rain in such torrents that it washed the trees from people's gardens and sent a wild river racing down through the valley. A flooded river, a swollen river, a river in spate.

The cobblestone maker thought: *Great. Now I'm important. Now I'm powerful. Now I'm strong. My wish has been granted. My ambition has been fulfilled.*

The river crashed into a granite moun-tain, splitting into two streams, one on each side of the mountain. Again the cobblestone maker cursed. A mountain is more important than a flooded river, he thought. So, if I want to be more important than that, I must wish to be a granite mountain.

As he made his wish, there was a flash of blue light, and the cobblestone maker became a granite mountain, standing four-square at the head of the valley. There he stayed as the days became weeks, the weeks became months and the months became years.

One morning, he woke with a tickling, itching on his back. He looked around and there, on the back of the mountain, chipping away patiently, was … a cobblestone maker.

Finally, the cobblestone maker realised that he *was* important: he didn't need to be a king, a cloud or even a mountain, because people rely on folk just like him to give them the things they need.

And so the one who chips away at the rocks is just as important as the one who builds the roads. And the one who cleans the hospitals is just as important as the one who performs the operations. And you are each as important as anyone else in this world.

The **Grasmere** Gingerbread Man

GRASMERE

Opposite the Storyteller's Garden is Sarah Nelson's famous gingerbread shop, because Grasmere is the gingerbread capital of the world! However, when the local children take part in the summer Rushbearing Festival, the gingerbread they are given is more like ginger cake, and is made by the village baker. This is his story.

One day, Colin the Baker was feeling lonely, so he mixed up a very special gingerbread dough. He took a handful of the mixture and rolled it into a sausage to make the body and put in on a tray. He rolled another handful into a ball and popped it above the body to make the head. He took one last handful and rolled it into a long thin sausage to make the arms and the legs. He put these in place and squashed it flat. Popping the tray into the oven, he went upstairs and had a cup of tea.

When he came down again, he could hear a tap-tap-tapping coming from inside the oven. He opened the oven door and, standing on the edge of the tray was the little gingerbread man, who jumped out and ran around the room saying, 'Run, run, as fast as you can, you can't catch me, I'm the Grasmere gingerbread man.'

Colin the Baker began to chase him.

And the gingerbread man said, 'Run, run, as fast as you can, you can't catch me, I'm the Grasmere gingerbread man.'

The little gingerbread man ran into a shop. Who should be in the shop but my two daughters, Aimee and Rosie. Aimee is a very good girl, but often leaves doors open. The gingerbread man ran out of the door, turned left and started running towards the Tourist Information Centre, chased by Aimee, Rosie and Colin the Baker.

And the little gingerbread man said, 'Run, run, as fast as you can, you can't catch me, I'm the Grasmere gingerbread man.'

The woman who works in the Tourist Information Centre is called Mrs Rickman. She raced out of the shop, and the grannies and grandpas came out of the old folks' home – some in their wheelchairs – and chased the gingerbread man towards St Oswald's Church. Running towards the church was Aimee, Rosie, Colin the Baker, Mrs Rickman and the grannies and grandpas in their wheelchairs.

The verger who looks after the church is called Bob and he has a big black dog called Sweep. When the dog saw the gingerbread man, he licked his chops and gave chase, pulling Bob along on the end of the lead. The gingerbread man headed towards the village school, chased by Aimee, Rosie, Colin the Baker, Mrs Rickman, the grannies and grandpas in their wheelchairs, Bob, and Sweep the dog.

And the gingerbread man said, 'Run, run, as fast as you can, you can't catch me, I'm the Grasmere gingerbread man.'

Mike the Headmaster was looking out of the window. He rushed out and joined the chase as the gingerbread man headed towards the Wordsworth Museum – Dove Cottage – once the home of the famous poet William Wordsworth, long ago. Running towards the museum was the gingerbread man, chased by Aimee, Rosie, Colin the Baker, Mrs Rickman, the grannies and grandpas in their wheelchairs, Bob, Sweep the Dog, and Mike the Headmaster. The curator of the museum is called Terry, and he has two boys, Rowan and Tangwyn. They came out and joined the chase.

The gingerbread man thought if he could cross Grasmere Lake, he could climb over Red Bank and escape into Langdale, the next valley. Running towards the lake was the gingerbread man, chased by Aimee, Rosie, Colin the Baker, Mrs Rickman, the grannies and grandpas in their wheelchairs, Bob, Sweep the Dog, Mike the Headmaster, Terry the Curator, Rowan and Tangwyn.

And the gingerbread man said, 'Run, run, as fast as you can, you can't catch me, I'm the Grasmere gingerbread man.'

Standing on the edge of the lake was a red-haired fox – a vixen. She licked her chops as the gingerbread man ran towards her.

'Can you swim?' asked the gingerbread man.

'Certainly,' said the vixen.

So the gingerbread man jumped on her back and she paddled into the lake. As she swam towards the island in the middle, the water splashed up the vixen's back, and the gingerbread man leapt on to her head. The gingerbread man was still getting splashed, and there is nothing worse than soggy gingerbread. He tugged her ears, pulling her nose towards the sky, and leapt on to the tip of it. He thought he was safe for he could see all the people who had chased him stuck on the shore, shaking their fists.

However, the vixen was hungry and the vixen was crafty: as she reached the island, she tossed her nose and flicked the gingerbread man into the air. As he fell she caught him in her jaws … and gobbled him all up!

The Giant
Hoad

ULVERSTON

Many places have stories that explain how rivers, mountains or even pubs came to get their names. Perhaps you know some from where you live. If somewhere has an unusual name, it is probably because of an old story. The Lake District is no exception, as in this area 'the legends grow out of the land'. These days if you visit Ulverston you can see Hoad Hill has a lighthouse monument on top of it. Thank goodness it wasn't there when the giant in the story that follows sat down on top of the hill!

A long time ago, when birds built their nests in old men's beards, a giant came from Scotland down to the Lake District. Tired from his journey, the giant looked for somewhere to sit and rest. The local people were terrified of him, partly because he was Scottish, but mainly because he was so huge.

Sitting on that hill, the giant realised he could paddle with one foot in Morecambe Bay and the other in the River Duddon. Peering over Morecambe Bay the Scotsman saw something he had never seen before. Where he'd come from in Scotland there were fishermen on the coast, but they all fished from boats with nets and lines. The fishermen of Morecambe Bay, however, didn't need boats. They used nets and lines, but the tide went out so far they could use horses to tow their nets. Also, there are very dangerous parts of the bay where patches of floating sand, called quicksand, can suck an animal or a person under and drown them. Actually, in the old days, entire coaches and horses sometimes disappeared in the sands of the bay.

The giant watched Joss Westmorland, a local fisherman, pulling his shrimp net behind a white horse and a black horse called Chalk and Cheese. Normally Joss knew the bay well and could guide his horses between the deadly patches of sinking sand. However, on this day Joss took the horses and net too close to one of the biggest patches of quicksand, where they all started to sink with a loud gurgling sound. In a matter of minutes both the horses and the fisherman were up to their chins in sand and water.

The giant stood up and took three great steps into the bay. Bending down, he picked up the horses and the net, which was full of shrimps, in his right hand, and Joss the fisherman in his left. The giant placed them back safely in their yard at Flookburgh before sitting back on his hill with a handful of shrimps to eat.

The giant had saved Morecambe Bay's favourite young fisherman, so the local people weren't frightened of him anymore. In fact, they named the hill after him. That giant's name was Angus Hoad, so ever since then that hill has been called Hoad Hill. Every Friday the locals bring him a basket of shrimps to eat. On Monday, when the people of Grange, Cartmel, Arnside and Ulverston hang their washing on their lines, they wave to the giant. When the giant waves back, he creates just enough breeze to dry their washing.

The Dragon
of Rydal Cave

RYDAL

Walkers following the footpath along the side of Loughrigg Fell, between Grasmere and Ambleside, are often surprised to come across a cave, high in the fell-side above Rydal Water. This cave was once the home of a dragon who loved stories.

There was once a young boy who lived in the 'valley where rye was grown' – otherwise known as Rydal. His name was George, and he loved to play the violin. Not only that, but he also loved walking on Loughrigg Fell above Rydal Water and Grasmere Lake. Now along this route there is a deep, dark cave.

One day, George sat on a rock by the opening of the cave and he played a beautiful tune on his violin.

At the end of the tune he heard a deep, silky voice which said, 'Thank you for that music. For that I will tell you a story.'

The voice of the creature – for George had no idea what it was – told a magical tale.

At the end of the story, George said, 'Thank you very much.'

The voice asked George if he would return again the following day to share another tune and a tale. In fact, it asked, might George consider returning every day for a tune and a tale?

George promised that he would.

And so it was that the following day, George swapped another tune for a tale from the soft, mysterious voice.

By the third or fourth day, young George was beginning to wonder who or what his new friend was.

As the sun dipped down in the sky, a shaft of sunlight shone into the mouth of the cave. Bravely, George stepped just inside the opening and looked up.

He was staring into two shining golden discs.

Looking down, he saw an enormous, green, scaly foot.

He was looking straight into the eyes of a dragon!

George said, 'So it's you who has been telling me stories.'

The dragon laughed, 'Aren't you afraid of me?'

'Why should I be afraid of you?' replied George. 'I play you music and you tell me stories, and we are friends.'

The dragon said, 'But I could crush you with one stamp of my foot, or I could fry you with one puff of my breath.'

Now it was George's turn to laugh. 'You wouldn't do that. We're friends.'

This made the dragon very happy.

He pleaded with George: 'Please, promise you'll come and visit every day or I will be lonely.'

George replied, 'If you're lonely why don't you come home with me and live in my village?'

'I couldn't possibly do that,' said the dragon. 'Your people would kill me, because for years we have been at war. Ever since your great-great-great-great-great-grandfather George fought my great-great-great-great-great-grandfather dragon, we have not been able to be friends. Not until now.'

Young George thought hard about this, and then he came up with an idea. He knew that the people of Rydal were worried. The crop had not been good and something had to be done.

So George said, 'If we had a story-teller in Rydal, then visitors and poets would come to our village and it would be famous. So why don't you come and be our storyteller?'

George promised he would have a word with the Lord of the Manor, LeFleming of Rydal Hall, and bring him to meet his dragon friend the following day.

The dragon said, 'Do you promise?' and young George, who knew the meaning of a promise, said, 'Yes.'

George went straight to the Lord's house and told him about his new friend and his brilliant idea. George told him that he would take him to meet the storyteller, but that he would have to be blindfolded as the storyteller was very shy.

LeFleming was astonished that there was such a thing as a shy storyteller!

The following day, the blindfolded LeFleming put his hands on young George's shoulders, and his entourage of servants, also blindfolded, put their hands on the Lord's shoulders.

They walked all the way up to the cave and stepped inside.

George whispered into the darkness, 'We've come.'

The deep silky voice said, 'You kept your promise,' and started to cry with happiness.

As he did so, one great silver tear fell from the dragon's eyes and landed on LeFleming's bald head. Feeling it drop, the Lord couldn't resist lifting his blindfold, and found himself gazing into the golden eyes of the dragon. The servants followed suit.

'Are **YOU** the storyteller?' asked LeFleming in amazement.

So in his deep silky voice, the dragon told them a wonderful tale of a promise kept, and to George's delight, the grown-ups asked the dragon if he would come and live with them in their village, and be their storyteller.

The dragon said he would be delighted to do just that.

Then the Lord said, 'Before you do, would you grant us one wish?'

'And what would that be?' asked the dragon, to which the Lord of the Manor said, 'Could we have a ride on your back?'

So George, the Lord of the Manor, and all the servants climbed on the dragon's back. He spread his leathery wings and soared high in the sky and circled above the beautiful lakes.

Eventually, young George and the Lord whispered in the dragon's ear that they must return to Rydal as they had a promise to keep. So the dragon landed safely down in the valley and his friends all went on their way.

The dragon lived happily in Rydal Cave for many years, going into the village every now and then to tell his stories. Just as George had hoped, the storyteller attracted visitors and poets from far and wide and Rydal village became famous.

And when the dragon died, he didn't die alone. He lay resting his head on the knee of a very old man called George, who had once been a little boy called George who had played him tunes in exchange for stories.

AND NOW A POEM
THE STORYTELLER

In the 1980s I had the pleasure of staying at the home of folk singer Mike Jones, his storyteller wife Joan and their daughter Sian. Over five days of schools and folk-club performances, my tales and introductions inspired Mike to put together the words overleaf. He sent me a handwritten copy of the finished version as a gift, hoping that I would like it. I really cherish that first copy and hope that you like it as much as I do.

Although created as a song, it stands as a poem encapsulating many of my thoughts on the art that I love and practise – that of storytelling.

THE STORYTELLER

I'm a teller of tales, a spinner
  of yarns,
A weaver of dreams and a liar.
I'll teach you some stories to tell to
  your friends,
While sitting at home by the fire.
You may not believe everything that
  I say
But there's one thing I'll tell you
  that's true,
For my stories were given as presents
  to me
And now they are my gifts
to you.

My stories are as old as the
  mountains and rivers
That flow through the land they
  were born in
They were told in the homes of
  peasants in rags
And kings with fine clothes adorning.
There's no need for silver or gold in
  great store
For a tale becomes richer with telling
And as long as each listener has a
  pair of good ears
It matters not where they are
  dwelling.

A story well told can lift up your
  hearts
And help you forget all your
  sorrows
It can give you the strength and the
  courage to stand
And face all your troubles tomorrow.
For there's wisdom and wit, beauty
  and charm
There's laughter and sometimes
  there's tears
But when the story is over and the
  spell it is broken
You'll find that there's nothing to fear

My stories were learned in my
grandparents' home
Where their grandparents also had
heard them
They were given as payment by
travelling folk
For a warm place to lay down their
burdens
My stories are ageless, they never
grow old
With each telling they are born anew
And when my story is ended, I'll
still be alive
In the tales that I've given to you.

...AND NOW FINALLY

Remember the riddle you solved to open this book? Now take the key and lock it again so that the stories don't escape until you next unlock it to visit them again.

The people in the stories are happy,
And so are we.
Let's put on the kettle,
We'll have a cup of tea.

Also from The History Press

Society *for* Storytelling

Since 1993, the Society for Storytelling has championed the art of oral storytelling and the benefits it can provide – such as improving memory more than rote learning, promoting healing by stimulating the release of neuropeptides, or simply great entertainment! Storytellers, enthusiasts and academics support and are supported by this registered charity to ensure the art is nurtured and developed throughout the UK.

Many activities of the Society are available to all, such as locating storytellers on the Society website, taking part in our annual National Storytelling Week at the start of every February, purchasing our quarterly magazine *Storylines*, or attending our Annual Gathering – a chance to revel in engaging performances, inspiring workshops, and the company of like-minded people.

You can also become a member of the Society to support the work we do. In return, you receive free access to *Storylines*, discounted tickets to the Annual Gathering and other storytelling events, the opportunity to join our mentorship scheme for new storytellers, and more. Among our great deals for members is a 30% discount off titles in the *Folk Tales* series from The History Press website.

For more information, including how to join, please visit

www.sfs.org.uk